*'A unique and extraordinary book.'*

Many of us will face a life-threatening illness at some time in our lives, or will lose someone close to us as a result of one.

Talking to children about a terminal diagnosis is one of the hardest things any parent can be faced with. This unique and extraordinary book has been created to help with that task.
There are many different ways to use and share it.

**Dr Konrad Jacobs**

Consultant Clinical Child Psychologist

Oxford University Hospitals

Author and illustrator royalties will be donated to the charities 'Mummy's Star' who support women and their families affected by cancer during pregnancy and 'We Hear You' (WHY), who give free professional counselling to those affected or bereaved by cancer or other life threatening conditions.

Only One of Me – Mum
Published in Great Britain in 2018 by Graffeg Limited. This paperback edition 2022.

ISBN 9781802581607

Written by Lisa Wells and Michelle Robinson copyright © 2018. Illustrated by Catalina Echeverri copyright © 2018. Designed and produced by Graffeg Limited copyright © 2018.

Graffeg Limited, 15 Neptune Court, Vanguard Way, Cardiff, CF24 5PJ, Wales, UK.
Tel: +44(0)1554 824000. www.graffeg.com.

Lisa Wells and Michelle Robinson are hereby identified as the authors of this work in accordance with section 77 of the Copyrights, Designs and Patents Act 1988.

# Only one of Me

A love letter from Mum

Written by Lisa Wells, Michelle Robinson    Illustrated by Catalina Echeverri

**GRAFFEG**

There's only one mum quite like me.

I wish that there were two.
I'd have more time to spend
And I would spend it all with you.

There's only one mum quite like me.
I wish that there were three.

We'd journey far together –
Oh, the places we would see!

There's only one mum
quite like me.

I wish there could be four.

I'd wrap my arms around you,
Keep you safe for ever more.

There's only one mum quite like me.
I'd sooner there were five.
I'd tell you how I love you
Every day I were alive.

But there is only one of me.
There aren't as many days
As I would want to spend with you,
In all those special ways...

To share the happy times with you,
To wipe away your tears,
To hold your hand and guide you
Through the weeks
and months and years.

To tell you, "I am proud of you."

To teach you, "You are strong."

To let you know, "I'll love you

Even after I am gone."

So I am asking Daddy
And I'm asking Auntie too,
Uncles, Grannies, Grandpas, friends –

Here's what you *all* must do:

19

Become a *little bit* like me –

Not *quite* like Mum, but try.

Help my children learn to live if one day I should die.

Give my child your time and love.
Lead them far and wide.

Keep them safe and hold them tight
Long after I have died.

They say that time will help you heal.
I say, *I'll* help you, too.
It's *me* who'll be behind the crowd
Of people helping *you*.

That is what I'm asking *them*.
I'll ask *you* something, too.
It's just a little something
That I'm certain you can do.

Don't worry if you cry a lot.

It's okay to get mad.

Even laughing's good –

There's more than one way to feel sad.

And be a little bit like Mum.

Be free!

Be brave!

Be kind!

Remember all our joy and fun

When you remember me.

Love you always,
Mummy xxx

# Lisa Wells

Lisa Wells was diagnosed with terminal bowel and liver cancer in December 2017. Determined to leave a legacy of love for five-year-old Ava-Lily and ten-month-old Saffia, she created Lisa's Army UK – a team of loved ones who will help support her husband Dan and the girls in a future Lisa won't live to see. Lisa has raised over £83k for charity and won Hello! Magazine's Star Mum Award. *Only One of Me* began as Lisa's love letter to her daughters. She hopes its publication will bring comfort to your family too. lisasarmy.co.uk

# Michelle Robinson

Michelle Robinson lives a few streets away from co-author Lisa in Frome, Somerset. Michelle's dad was diagnosed with bowel cancer in 2016.

Meeting and working with Lisa has been the highlight of Michelle's career to date – even topping the time Tim Peake read her book *Goodnight Spaceman* to Earth from space. Michelle's many other books include *Ten Fat Sausages*, *How To Wash a Woolly Mammoth* and *Tooth Fairy In Training*. michellerobinson.co.uk

# Catalina Echeverri

Catalina Echeverri was born in Bogota, Colombia and is mum to a little daughter. Catalina studied Graphic Design in Milano, Italy and Children's Book Illustration in Cambridge, England before settling in London.

She has worked with both national and international clients and her book *There's a Dinosaur in my Bathtub* was shortlisted for the AOI Illustration Awards. cataecheverri.com

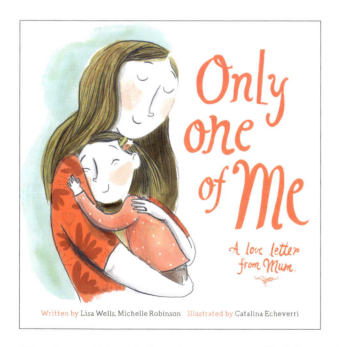

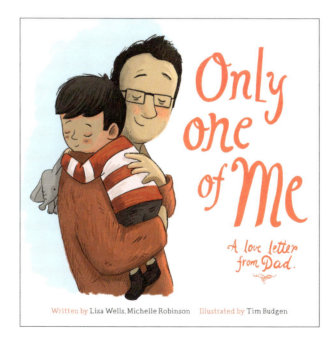

Copies of both books are available at bookshops and also www.graffeg.com